My Weirder S...

Miss Kraft Is Daft!

Dan Gutman

Pictures by
Jim Paillot

HARPER

An Imprint of HarperCollins Publishers

To Tony Grisolano

My Weirder School #7: Miss Kraft Is Daft!

Text copyright © 2013 by Dan Gutman

Illustrations copyright © 2013 by Jim Paillot

All rights reserved. Printed in the United States of America.

No part of this book may be used or reproduced in any manner whatsoever without written permission except in the case of brief quotations embodied in critical articles and reviews. For information address HarperCollins Children's Books, a division of HarperCollins Publishers, 10 East 53rd Street, New York, NY 10022.

www.harpercollinschildrens.com

Library of Congress Cataloging-in-Publication Data is available.

ISBN 978-0-06-204216-3 (lib. bdg.) — ISBN 978-0-06-204215-6 (pbk.)

Typography by Kate Engbring

13 14 15 16 17   CG/BR   10 9 8 7 6 5 4 3 2 1

❖

First Edition

Contents

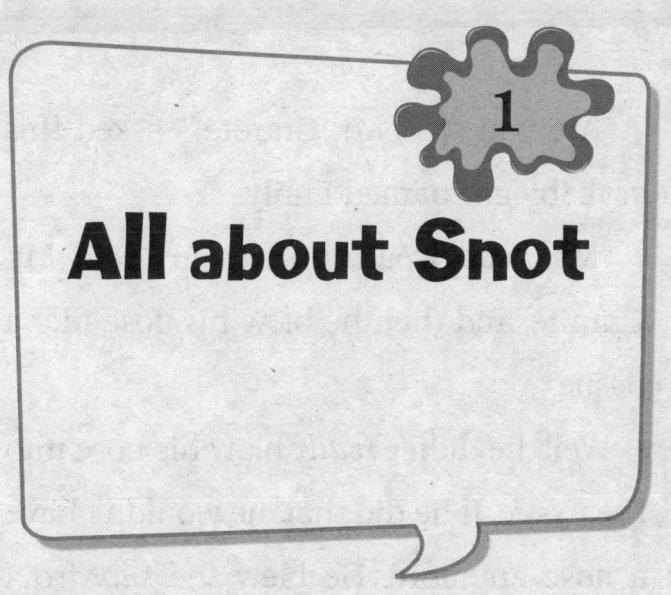

All about Snot

My name is A.J. and I hate snot.

Isn't snot gross? Liquid gunk comes out of your *nose*! How could it *not* be gross?

Last week my teacher, Mr. Granite, who is from another planet, came to school sneezing, wheezing, and coughing. His nose was red. He looked terrible.

"Are you sick, Mr. Granite?" asked this crybaby girl named Emily.

"My head is all stuffed up," said Mr. Granite, and then he blew his nose into a tissue.

Well, he didn't *really* blow his nose into the tissue. If he did that, he wouldn't have a nose anymore. He blew the *snot* from his nose into a tissue. Then he threw the tissue into the garbage can.

Ewwww! I thought I was gonna throw up. That's almost as disgusting as blowing the snot *straight* into the garbage can!*

"Excuse me," Mr. Granite said, "I need to

---

*Warning: This chapter is inappropriate for children. And grown-ups.

go get more tissues."

While Mr. Granite was out of the room, the class had a very interesting discussion.

"If your head is all stuffed up," asked Alexia, this girl who rides a skateboard all the time, "I guess that means your head is full of snot."

"No, it's not," I said. "Get it? No, it's snot?"

Nobody laughed at my joke, so I pretended that I never made it. If you ever tell a joke and nobody laughs, just pretend that you never made the joke and keep talking. That's the first rule of being a kid.

"A head can't be full of snot," I explained, "because if it was full of snot, there would be no room for your brain."

"That wouldn't be a problem with *you*," said Andrea, this annoying girl with curly brown hair, "because you don't *have* a brain!"

"Oh, snap!" said Ryan, who will eat anything, even stuff that isn't food.

"Your *face* doesn't have a brain," I told Andrea.

I knew that didn't make any sense, but I couldn't think of anything else to say.

"Maybe our heads are always making *more* snot," said Michael, who never ties his shoes.

"Or maybe our brain takes up half of our head, and the other half is made of snot," said Neil, who we call the nude kid even though he wears clothes.

"Maybe our brains turn *into* snot as we get older," I suggested. "So when we get *really* old, our heads are *completely* full of snot."

We had to end this discussion because Mr. Granite came back into the class with a box of tissues. He was still sniffling as we pledged the allegiance and did Word of the Day.

"Let's get to work," said Mr. Granite. "Turn to page twenty-three in your math books."

Ugh. I hate math. I'll do *anything* to get out of math.

Mr. Granite made a big honking noise with his nose.

"Maybe you should go home, Mr. Granite," I suggested. "You'll feel a lot better."

(And we won't have to do math!)

"Nice try, A.J.," he replied. "Page twenty-three is my favorite math lesson. But every time I try to work on it with you kids, we get called to an assembly. Well, I checked, and there's no assembly today. I'm not going to let a little cold stop me from—"

He didn't get the chance to finish his sentence because an announcement came over the loudspeaker.

"All classes, please report to the all-purpose room for a surprise assembly."

"Not again!" shouted Mr. Granite.

He was so mad, I thought he might jump out the window.

No More
Mr. Nice Guy

We had to walk a million hundred miles to the all-purpose room for the surprise assembly. I don't know why they call it the *all*-purpose room, because you can't use it for bungee jumping.

Our principal, Mr. Klutz, was up on the stage with our vice principal, Mrs. Jafee, and our school counselor, Dr. Brad. They're usually smiling and giving us high fives when we walk in for an assembly. But not this time. All three of them had on mean faces.

"What's up with *them*?" I whispered as we sat down.

"It looks like they got up on the wrong side of the bed," whispered Andrea.

"What difference does it make which side of the bed you get up on?" I asked.

"It's just an expression, Arlo," said Andrea, rolling her eyes. She calls me by my real name because she knows I don't like it.

"Maybe somebody died," whispered Ryan.

Mr. Klutz, Mrs. Jafee, and Dr. Brad were all wearing T-shirts that said BOGS on them.

"What do you think BOGS stands for?" whispered Neil the nude kid.

"Big Ostriches Go Slow," guessed Ryan.

"Boring Old Geezer Society," guessed Michael.

"Body Odor Gets Stinky," guessed Alexia.

"Be on Guard—"

I didn't get the chance to finish my sentence because Mr. Klutz held up his hand and made the shut-up peace sign. Mrs. Jafee tapped on the microphone. Everybody stopped talking. It was so quiet in the all-purpose room, you could hear a pin drop.

That is, if anybody brought pins to school and started dropping them. But why would anybody do a dumb thing like that?

"We are disappointed in you children," said Mrs. Jafee. "Once again, Dirk School got the award for having the best behavior of the month."

Dirk School is on the other side of town. That's where all the genius kids go. We call it "Dork School."

Mrs. Jafee sat down, and Dr. Brad stepped up to the microphone.

"We have been having a lot of behavior problems lately," he said. "Students have been yelling and running through the hallways. Kids are talking back to their teachers. There have been food fights and riots. This is *not* the way children are supposed to behave in school. So we're starting a program to improve behavior and teach respect here at Ella Mentry School."

Dr. Brad sat down, and Mr. Klutz stepped up to the microphone. He has no hair at all. I mean *none*. Mr. Klutz's head is really shiny. They could use it to signal ships that are lost at sea.

"BOGS stands for Behave or Get Suspended," said Mr. Klutz. "I've tried to be kind to you children, but it didn't work. So from now on, it's no more Mr. Nice Guy. Students who misbehave will be suspended."

Wow! I remember when Mr. Klutz was a good guy. One time I got sent to his office for bad behavior, and he gave me a candy bar. That was cool. Now he's all mean.

"I expect exemplary behavior at Ella Mentry School," he continued, "and that is all I have to say. I will be checking in on your classrooms regularly to see how you're making out."

"Ewwwwwww, disgusting!" I shouted. "Mr. Klutz said 'making out'!"

"QUIET!" roared Mr. Klutz. "Enough of that foolishness!"

Mr. Granite Is Dying!

We had to walk a million hundred miles back to class in single file. Everybody was being really quiet. Nobody wanted to get in trouble with Mr. Klutz. I looked around for Mr. Granite, but I couldn't find him.

When we passed the front office, our school nurse, Mrs. Cooney, pulled me out of the line. She is beautiful and has eyes that look like cotton candy. One time she wanted me to marry her, but I couldn't because she was already married to some guy named Mr. Cooney.

"A.J.," she whispered, "please tell your class that Mr. Granite went home for the rest of the day."

"Is he going to be okay?" I asked.

"Oh yes," said Mrs. Cooney. "He only has a cold."

I ran to catch up with the rest of the class. They were just going into our room, and everybody was still on their best behavior. Even the guys folded their hands on their desks and kept their feet

on the floor. It was weird.

"Where's Mr. Granite?" Neil the nude kid whispered to me.

"Mr. Granite has a cold," I whispered, "so he went home for the rest of the day. Spread the word."

Neil turned around and whispered to Emily. "Mr. Granite is old, so he went home for the rest of the day."

Emily opened her eyes really wide. Then she turned around and whispered to Ryan. "Mr. Granite is old, so he went to a rest home," she said.

Ryan leaned over to whisper to Michael. "Old Mr. Granite was put in a home for the rest of his life."

Michael turned around and whispered to Andrea. "Mr. Granite was put in an old-age home to rest until he's dead!"

"MR. GRANITE IS DYING?!" shouted Andrea.

Suddenly, everyone started yelling, screaming, crying, and freaking out.

"But Mr. Granite is so *young*!" wailed Michael.

"He was such a good man!" groaned Neil the nude kid.

"I need to speak with a grief counselor!" screamed Emily.

"Why? Why? Why?" everybody was moaning.

Kids were weeping, holding their heads, and wiping their eyes. The girls were talking about what they were going to wear to Mr. Granite's funeral.

That's when Mr. Klutz came running into the classroom like his hair was on fire.*

"What's the matter?" he shouted. "Is someone hurt?"

"Mr. Granite is dying!" yelled Andrea.

"No he's not," said Mr. Klutz. "He has a cold, so he went home for the rest of the day. Who told you that he's dying?"

---

*That is, if he had any hair. Hey, maybe that's how he lost his hair in the first place!

Ryan looked at me. Alexia looked at me. Michael looked at me. Emily looked at me. Everybody was looking at me.

"A.J. told us that Mr. Granite is dying!" Andrea said, pointing at me.

"I did not!"

"You did too!"

"Did not!"

"Did too!"

We went on like that for a while until Mr. Klutz clapped his hands together: *CLAP CLAP, CLAPCLAPCLAP.*

Five claps means "shut up." Nobody knows why.

"Remember what I said about your behavior," said Mr. Klutz as he left the room. "If you kids can't behave, some of you are going to be suspended. I'm not fooling around!"

It Takes Brains to Be a Sub

You know what it means when your teacher gets sick? It means you get a *substitute* teacher!

Yay!

Having a sub is cool because you don't have to do work or learn anything. You can do whatever you want. It's too bad teachers can't be sick *all* the time. Then school would be fun.

I pulled out a comic book and put my feet up on my desk. This was going to be the greatest day of my life.

But you'll never believe who ran into the door at that moment.

It was a lady dressed up like a clown and riding a unicycle! She ran right into the door!

"Ouch!" said the clown lady as she got up off the floor. "That hurt!"

Everybody laughed, because it's always hilarious when people crash into things and fall down. Nobody knows why. If you ask me, there should be a TV station that shows nothing but people crashing into things and falling down all day long. That would be cool.

"Hi boys and girls!" the clown lady said.

"My name is Miss Kraft."

"Are you a clown or a teacher?" asked Andrea.

"Both!" said Miss Kraft. "I'm a clown *and* a teacher. We're going to have fun and learn at the same time!"

"That's impossible," I said.

"Don't be a Grumpy Gus!" said Miss Kraft. "Watch *this*! What's two times one?"

"Two!" we all shouted.

Miss Kraft put her hand up to her face. Then she pulled a red handkerchief and a blue handkerchief out of her nose.

"And what's two times two?" she asked.

"Four!" we all shouted.

Miss Kraft pulled four colorful

handkerchiefs out of her nose.

"And what's two times three?" she asked.

"Six!" we all shouted.

Miss Kraft pulled *six* colorful handkerchiefs out of her nose. It was amazing!

"WOW!" we all shouted, which is "MOM" upside down.

"How did you fit all those handkerchiefs in your nose?" asked Ryan.

"Easy!" said Miss Kraft. "I took my brain out."

She reached into her pocket, and you'll never believe in a million hundred years what she had in there.

A brain!

"Eeeeeeeeeeeeeek!" everybody screamed,

even the guys.

Emily, the big crybaby, was hiding under her desk.

"What's the matter?" Miss Kraft asked her.

"I'm afraid of clowns," Emily said, whimpering. "Clowns are creepy."

Well, she's right about that. Clowns *are* creepy. Nobody knows why.

"There's nothing to be afraid of," Miss Kraft said. "Would anybody else like me to take out their brain?"

"Me! Me! Me!" shouted all the boys.

Miss Kraft went over to Michael and put her hand on the back of his head. When she pulled it away, she had *another* brain in her hand.

"Eeeeeeeeeeeeeeeeek!"

Emily freaked and went running out of the room. Sheesh, get a grip! That girl will fall for anything.

"You should take out A.J.'s brain, Miss Kraft," said Andrea. "He never uses it."

"Oh, snap!" said Ryan.

"Yeah, take out my brain!" I said.

Miss Kraft came over to me and put her hand on the back of my head. When she pulled it away, she had a *third* brain in her hand. Then she threw all the brains up in the air and started to juggle them.

"Look!" said Miss Kraft. "I'm juggling brains!"

Clowns are weird.

Clowning Around

Miss Kraft was still juggling the three brains when Mr. Klutz came in.

"Ah, I see you've met your substitute teacher," he said. "Miss Kraft just graduated from clown college."

"They have colleges for *clowns*?!" asked Alexia.

"Oh yes," said Miss Kraft. "This year I took classes in magic tricks, unicycle riding, and advanced balloon animals."

"Cool!" we all said.

"When I get bigger, I want to go to clown college," I said.

"I'm sure your parents will be happy to hear that, A.J.," said Mr. Klutz. "I just wanted to come in to assure you kids that Mr. Granite is fine and will be back tomorrow. Until then, I expect you all to be on your best behavior, just like you would be if Mr. Granite was here."

"I'm *always* on my best behavior," said Andrea.

What is her problem?

"Good," said Mr. Klutz, "because I know what happens when there's a substitute in the class. I was a boy once, you know."

"Just once?" I asked. "I'm a boy *all* the time."

"No, I mean that I used to be your age," he told us, "and we used to give the subs a hard time. But if there is going to be any bad behavior in here, there are going to be suspensions."

Mr. Klutz left the room.

"Hey, do you kids want to see a cool magic trick?" asked Miss Kraft.

"Yeah!" we all yelled.

"Watch me pull a rabbit out of my hat!"

"You don't have a hat," said Ryan.

"Oh, you're right," said Miss Kraft. "Then watch me pull a hat out of my rabbit."

She waved her arm around, and suddenly there was a big puff of smoke. When the smoke cleared, she was holding a rabbit!

"It's adorable!" yelled all the girls.

Then Miss Kraft waved her arm around again, and there was another puff of smoke. When the smoke cleared, she was holding a big top hat. The rabbit climbed out of it.

"WOW!" we all said, which as you know is "MOM" upside down.

Miss Kraft did some card tricks and coin tricks for us. Then she sang a song while she played a banjo. After that she did a funny clown dance, gave us candy, and made us some balloon animals.

Miss Kraft is cool! This was even *better* than having a regular sub. We didn't have to do any schoolwork; *plus* they brought in a clown to entertain us. Having Miss Kraft as a sub is like going to a birthday party all day long.

"Is everyone having fun?" she asked.

"Yeah!" we all yelled.

"I wish you were our teacher *every* day!" I told her.*

---

*Do you want to know the surprise ending? Well, I'm not going to tell you. So nah-nah-nah boo-boo on you!

The Big Bang

6

Miss Kraft is the coolest sub in the history of the world. We were going to play games, eat junk food, and have fun all day long.

"What are we going to do *now*, Miss Kraft?" asked Alexia.

"Yeah, are you going to make more balloon animals?" asked Ryan.

"No," said Miss Kraft.

"Are you going to give us candy and cookies?" asked Michael.

"No," said Miss Kraft.

"Are you going to ride your unicycle and juggle some more?" asked Emily.

"No," said Miss Kraft.

"Then what are we going to do?" I asked.

"Turn to page twenty-three in your math books," she said.

"WHAT!?"

I think my jaw dropped open, and my eyes popped out of my head like in the cartoons.

"B-b-but," I stuttered, "I thought we were going to play games and have fun today."

"We *played* games," Miss Kraft said. "We *had* fun. Now it's time to learn something."

Noooooooooo! This simply could not be happening!

I looked at the loudspeaker on the wall. I was sure we would get called to a surprise assembly. Or maybe there would be a fire drill. Or maybe an asteroid would destroy the earth, and school would be canceled for the rest of our lives. Something was *sure* to happen so we wouldn't have to do page twenty-three.

But nothing happened. We all pulled our math books out of our desks.

"Yay," said Andrea. "I *love* math!"

Why can't a truck full of math books fall on Andrea's head?

"Are you *really* going to teach us page twenty-three?" asked Neil the nude kid.

"Of course not!" said Miss Kraft. "I don't know anything about math. Mr. Bongo is going to teach you page twenty-three."

"Who's Mr. Bongo?" we all asked.

Miss Kraft pulled a white sock out of her pocket and put it on her hand.

"This is Mr. Bongo," she said. "He's my friend."

Sock puppets are weird. Whoever thought up the idea of making puppets

out of socks was a dumb-head. And I'll tell you, this was the lamest sock puppet in the history of the world. It was basically a sock with two big, googly eyes on it. "Hi kids!" said Mr. Bongo, even though we could totally see Miss Kraft's lips moving. "Turn to page twenty-three in your math books."

I opened my math book and turned to page twenty-three. That's when I saw these horrible words . . .

THE ELEVEN TIMES TABLE

Noooooooooooooooooooo!

Not the eleven times table! *Anything* but the eleven times table!

Mr. Granite taught us all the times tables up to ten. But he never got to page twenty-three. I always wondered what was on page twenty-three. And now I found out the horrible truth.

My friend Billy, who lives around the corner, told me that the times tables can only go up to ten. Billy said that if you try to multiply numbers higher than ten, the earth will fall off its axis. And if you get all the way up to eleven times eleven, you get sucked into a parallel universe, and you travel back in time until you get to the Big Bang, when your head explodes.

Billy knows all about stuff like that. He told me he knew a kid who tried to multiply eleven times eleven, and the kid's head exploded. That is a true fact. I told everybody on the playground about it.

"Okay, let's get started," said Mr. Bongo. "One times eleven equals eleven. That's easy, right?"

"Are you sure you want to do this?" I

asked Miss Kraft.

"Don't talk to *me* about it," said Miss Kraft. "Talk to Mr. Bongo. He's the one who's teaching the lesson."

"Two times eleven equals twenty-two," said Mr. Bongo, "because eleven added to eleven equals twenty-two."

"We really shouldn't be doing this," said Michael. "It's very dangerous."

"Three times eleven equals thirty-three," said Mr. Bongo.

"I have to go to the bathroom," said Ryan.

"Later," said Miss Kraft.

"Four times eleven equals forty-four," said Mr. Bongo.

"I'm scared!" said Emily.

"Five times eleven equals fifty-five," said Mr. Bongo.

"If he gets to eleven times eleven," I whispered to Ryan, "we're going to get sucked into a parallel universe and travel through time until our heads explode!"

"Six times eleven equals sixty-six," said Mr. Bongo.

"Make him stop!" begged Neil the nude kid. "Please, make him stop!"

"Seven times eleven equals seventy-seven," said Mr. Bongo.

"He's getting close to the end!" said Andrea.

"Eight times eleven equals eighty-eight," said Mr. Bongo.

"I want my mommy!" said Emily, who

was hiding under her desk.

"Nine times eleven equals ninety-nine," said Mr. Bongo.

"Help!" shouted Ryan. "I'm too young to die!"

"Ten times eleven equals a hundred and ten," said Mr. Bongo.

"Good-bye, cruel world!" shouted Michael.

Everybody was hiding under their desks, holding their hands over their ears and freaking out.

"Eleven times eleven equals . . ."

"This is it!" I yelled, closing my eyes. "I'm going to miss you guys!"

". . . a hundred and twenty-one," said Mr. Bongo.

**11 × 11
equals...**

I felt my head to see if it had exploded.
All the pieces seemed to be there. I peeked
through my fingers to see if the world was
still there.

Nothing happened. The only thing that was different was that Mr. Klutz was standing in the doorway.

"What's the meaning of this?" he yelled. "Why are you children hiding under your desks during a math lesson?"

"We don't want to get sucked into a parallel universe," I explained.

Mr. Klutz looked really mad. I thought he was going to suspend the whole class. But he just turned around and stormed down the hall.

Okay, so my friend Billy was wrong. We didn't get sucked into a parallel universe and travel through time until our heads exploded.

I still say sock puppets are weird.

The Truth about Miss Kraft

After we finished the math lesson, it was time for lunch. We had to walk in single file a million hundred miles to the vomitorium.

I sat with Alexia and the guys, but Andrea and Emily weaseled their way onto the end of our table. They are so annoying.

We all had peanut butter and jelly sandwiches except for Ryan. He had a turkey wichsand, which is a sandwich that has the meat on the outside and bread in the middle.

"Miss Kraft is weird," I said.

"Yeah, I thought she was going to be cool when she was doing all that clown stuff," said Michael. "But then she made us do math."

"She's just like every other teacher," said Alexia. "All she ever wants to do is teach us stuff."

"Yeah, she's no fun at all," I said.

That's when Little Miss Know-It-All had to open her big mouth.

"Learning is a *good* thing, you know,"

Andrea said. "When you learn new things, it makes you a better person."

"Can you possibly be more boring?" asked Alexia.

Andrea and Alexia started sticking their tongues out at each other, which is what you do when somebody says something mean to you.

Little Miss Perfect was getting on my nerves. I tried to think of something I could do that would annoy her. So I picked up two straws and put them in my nostrils.

"Look, I'm a walrus!" I announced. Everybody laughed, except for Andrea, of course.

"That's disgusting, Arlo," she said.

"So is your face," I told her.

"Oh, snap!" said Ryan.

I was going to put two more straws into my ears, but you'll never believe in a million hundred years who came over to our table at that moment.

It was Mr. Klutz! He looked a little happier than before. But just to be on the safe side, I pulled the straws out of my nostrils and threw them under the table.*

"Hi everybody!" said Mr. Klutz. "I just wanted to see how you were making out with Miss Kraft."

"Ewwwwww, gross!" I said. "We weren't making out with Miss Kraft!"

"Isn't she a great teacher?" asked Mr. Klutz.

"Miss Kraft is *wonderful*!" said Andrea. "She makes learning fun."

Mr. Klutz liked hearing that, and he went to ask the kids at the other tables how much they liked making out with Miss Kraft.

---

*The straws, that is, not my nostrils. It would be weird to throw your nostrils under a table.

"I was just thinking," I told everybody after he left, "maybe Miss Kraft isn't a real substitute teacher at all."

"What do you mean?" asked Alexia.

"Well," I said, "maybe she's just a clown who ran away from the circus."

"People don't run away from the circus," Ryan told me. "They run away from home to *join* the circus."

"Well, what about this," I suggested. "Maybe Miss Kraft murdered our *real* substitute teacher at the circus and came to our school so nobody would know what happened."

"Then she would get away with murder!" Neil said.

"I saw that in a movie once," said Michael. "A guy murdered somebody, and then he pretended to be the guy he murdered so nobody would know the guy was missing."

"That's ridiculous!" Andrea said, rolling her eyes. "You're just trying to scare Emily."

"I'm scared!" said Emily.

"A.J. may be right," said Alexia. "I don't think Miss Kraft is a real substitute teacher."

"What if she didn't murder our real sub," I suggested. "What if she *kidnapped* our real substitute teacher and has her locked up at the circus, in a cage with a lion? Stuff like that happens all the time, you know."

"Yeah," said Michael, "and the lion is probably pacing back and forth right now, wondering why a substitute teacher is in its cage."

"I bet that lion is hungry," said Ryan.

"We've got to *do* something!" shouted Emily, and then she went running out of the vomitorium.

Sheesh! That girl will fall for *anything*.

After Emily left, Alexia told us that at her old school the kids used to play tricks on the substitute teachers.

"What kind of tricks?" I asked, instantly interested.

"Like, we would all drop our books on

the floor at the same time," she said. "The substitute teacher would be talking, and then suddenly, there was a loud *boom*. It was hilarious."

"We should do that!" said Ryan.

"Yeah," said Michael. "That would be cool!"

"I'm not going to do that," said Andrea. "You heard what Mr. Klutz said about behavior. You're going to get in trouble. You might get suspended."

"Not if we *all* do it," said Alexia. "They can't punish *all* of us."

Everybody except for Andrea agreed that dropping our books at the same time was a great idea and that Alexia should get the No Bell Prize. That's a prize they give out to people who don't have bells.

"Let's all drop our books on the floor at exactly one o'clock," Alexia said.

It was going to be hilarious. I couldn't wait for one o'clock to come.

The Great Kraftini

When we got back to class after lunch, Miss Kraft was wearing a top hat and a black cape. That was weird.

I looked at the clock. It was twelve thirty—just a half an hour until the Big Book Drop.

"Did you have a nice lunch, Miss Kraft?"

asked Andrea, the big brownnoser.

"Who's Miss Kraft?" asked Miss Kraft. "I'm The Great Kraftini! Watch *this*!"

She snapped her fingers. There was a big puff of smoke, and the empty desk in front of the room disappeared.

"Cool!" we all yelled.

"How did you do that?" asked Alexia.

"Oh, a magician never reveals her secrets," said Miss Kraft.

"Can you make Andrea disappear?" I asked.

"Oh, snap!" said Ryan.

"That's mean, Arlo!" said Andrea.

"Kids learn fast when you combine teaching with magic," Miss Kraft told us.

"Here, I'll show you. Grab this rope, A.J., and tie me up."

"Tie you up?" I asked. "Are you *sure*?"

"Sure I'm sure," said Miss Kraft. "Go ahead. Make it really tight."

I wrapped the thick rope around and around Miss Kraft until she was completely wrapped up from head to toe. Then I tied the ends together tightly. There was no way she could escape.

"Excuse me," said Andrea. "What could we possibly learn from *this*?"

"A lot!" said Miss Kraft. "While I try to escape from the ropes, I want you kids to write down the fifty American states in ABC order. If I can't escape in five minutes or you don't have the states in order, a five-hundred-pound weight will fall on my head."

We all looked up at the ceiling. There was a big weight hanging over Miss Kraft's head!*

Miss Kraft is daft!

"That's crazy!" yelled Neil the nude kid.

"Please don't do this, Miss Kraft," begged Emily. "It's very dangerous."

"I must do it," said Miss Kraft. "It's the only way you will learn. Hurry! The clock is ticking!"

"Alabama!" Ryan shouted. "The first state is Alabama! Somebody write it down!"

---

*Ask your teacher if you can try this at *your* school!

Emily grabbed a sheet of paper and a pencil. Everybody started yelling out states.

"Alaska!" yelled Andrea. "It's Alabama, Alaska . . . Arizona . . . Arkansas. . . . What's next?"

"Wyoming!" I yelled.

"No, dumbhead," said Andrea. "Wyoming comes *last.*"

"I knew that," I lied.

"California!" shouted Michael. "The next state is California! And then comes Colorado and Connecticut!"

Emily wrote the states down as fast as she could. Miss Kraft struggled to free herself from the ropes, but I had wrapped them pretty tightly.

"Four minutes left!" shouted Alexia.

We racked our brains to put the states in ABC order: Delaware, Florida, Georgia, Hawaii, Idaho. This was hard to do!

"Hurry!" Emily shouted. "Three minutes left!"

Everybody was freaking out. We got

Illinois, Indiana, Iowa, and Kansas. Miss Kraft couldn't get free from the ropes. She was grunting and sweating.

"Kentucky!" Andrea shouted. "Then comes Louisiana!"

"Two minutes left!" shouted Neil.

We got all the *M* states: Maine, Maryland, Massachusetts, Michigan, Minnesota, Mississippi, Missouri, and Montana.

"One minute left!" Ryan shouted. "Hurry!"

"Nebraska and Nevada!" shouted Alexia.

"And then all those "New" states!" shouted Neil. "New Hampshire, New Jersey, New Mexico, and New York!"

We were running out of time, and there

were still a lot of states left. In a few seconds the five-hundred-pound weight was going to drop on Miss Kraft's head!

"North Carolina!" Andrea shouted. "North Dakota! Ohio! Oklahoma!"

"Five seconds left!" shouted Ryan.

"There's no more time!" shouted Andrea.

"Oh *nooooooooooooooo*!"

I closed my eyes so I wouldn't have to see the five-hundred-pound weight fall on Miss Kraft's head.

That's when the most amazing thing in the history of the world happened. You'll never believe who walked into the door at that moment.

Nobody! It would hurt if you walked

into a door.

But you'll never believe who walked into the *doorway*. It was Mr. Klutz!

"What's going on in here?!" he hollered. "Why is Miss Kraft tied up with rope? Who did this to her?!"

Everybody looked at me.

"A.J.!" shouted Mr. Klutz. "Why would you tie up your teacher with ropes? Is that any way to show respect to a substitute? What did I tell you about behavior?"

"B-b-b-but . . . ," I said.

Everybody started giggling because I said "but," which sounds just like "butt" even though it has one less *t*.

"I'm keeping an eye on you, young

man!" yelled Mr. Klutz. "You are *this* close to being suspended."

I wanted to go to Antarctica and live with the penguins.

The Big Book Drop

"Oh, don't worry about *him*," said Miss Kraft after Mr. Klutz left the room. "I know how to take care of principals."

She also told us the five-hundred-pound weight wasn't *really* going to drop on her head, and it wasn't five hundred pounds either. It was made out of cardboard. She said she knew we would put the states in ABC order faster if we thought a five-hundred-pound weight was about to drop on her head.

Ryan and I untied the ropes around Miss Kraft.

So she had played a little trick on us. That was okay, because we were about to play a little trick on *her*.

I looked at the clock. It was 12:45. Fifteen minutes until the Big Book Drop.

"Okay, everybody!" Miss Kraft said. "It's D.E.A.R. time!"

D.E.A.R. stands for Drop Everything and Read. We all have to read silently for half an hour. Ugh, I hate reading.

We all took books out from our desks. I had a book about fighter planes that I got from the school library. Reading it wasn't much fun, but the pictures of the fighter planes were cool.

It was hard to concentrate on my book anyway, because all I could think about was the Big Book Drop. I checked the clock. Ten minutes to go.

I turned around to look at Ryan, Michael, Neil, and all the other kids. Everybody was reading silently. Miss Kraft was sitting at Mr. Granite's desk, reading a book called *Magic Tricks for Dummies*.

I moved my pile of books to the edge of my desk so it would be easier to drop them on the floor. It was going to be hilarious when we all dropped our books at the same time.

Five minutes to go.

I could barely even look at my book about fighter planes. It was almost one o'clock. Out of the corner of my eye, I saw Ryan passing a note to Michael. I figured he was reminding Michael to drop his books at one o'clock.

There were only a few minutes left. Kids were snickering and whispering and passing notes back and forth.

I looked at the second hand on the clock. It was sweeping around the dial. This was going to be *hilarious*!

The second hand was getting close to the top. Twelve seconds left!

I got ready for the Big Book Drop.

10 ... 9 ... 8 ... 7 ... 6 ...

It was so exciting!

5 ... 4 ... 3 ... 2 ... 1!

One o'clock! It was time! I pushed the pile of books off my desk.

Boom!

My books hit the floor. Miss Kraft jumped in her seat.

Ahahahahahahaha!

I looked around. Nobody else had dropped their books on the floor.

WHAT?!

Everybody was looking at me.

I probably don't need to tell you who walked into the doorway at that moment.

It was Mr. Klutz, of course.

"What was that loud bang?" he asked.

"Arlo dropped a bunch of books on the floor," Andrea said, a little smile on her face.

"Why did you do *that*, A.J.?" asked Mr. Klutz. He looked mad.

"I-I thought *everybody* was going to drop their books at one o'clock," I explained. "That was the plan."

"The *plan*?" said Mr. Klutz. "You *planned* to have everyone drop their books on the floor? Is that your idea of *fun*? One more stunt like that and you will be suspended, young man!"

"B-b-b-but . . ."

Everybody started giggling because I said "but" again.

Getting Suspended

Wow, Mr. Klutz was *really* mad. And so was I. When we went out for recess, I gave everybody a piece of my mind.

Well, I didn't *really* give them a piece of my mind. If I did that, I would have less mind for myself. But I told them how angry I was.

"How come you guys didn't drop your books on the floor at one o'clock?" I asked. "That was the plan!"

"We chickened out," Ryan told me, "so we called off the Big Book Drop."

"Why didn't anybody tell *me* you called off the Big Book Drop?" I asked them.

"I thought *you* told A.J.," Ryan said to Michael.

"I thought *you* told A.J.," Michael said to Neil.

"I thought *you* told A.J.," Neil said to Alexia.

"I thought *you* told A.J.," Alexia said to Ryan.

"*Nobody* told me!" I yelled at them. "And now if I do one more bad thing, I'm going to get suspended."

"What does being suspended mean anyway?" asked Alexia.

"It means you get kicked out of school," I told her.

"Kicked out of school?" she said. "So

you won't have to go to school anymore?"

"That's right."

"Hey, that means you get to stay home and watch TV," Ryan told me.

"It sounds pretty good to me," said Michael.

"Yeah," said Neil. "I wish I could get suspended. You're lucky, A.J."

"That can't be right," said Alexia. "Are you *sure* that being suspended means you get to stay home and watch TV?"

That's when Emily and Little Miss I-Know-Everything walked by.

"Hey Andrea," shouted Ryan. "You know everything. What does being suspended mean?"

"I'll look it up!" Andrea said cheerfully.

She reached into her pocket and pulled out a little dictionary. I guess she carries it with her wherever she goes so she can look up words and show everybody how smart she is.

Andrea leafed through her dictionary for a minute until she found the right page.

"Ah, here it is," she said. "'Suspend. To hang.' Suspend means 'to hang.'"

"So if A.J. does one more bad thing," Neil said, "Mr. Klutz is going to *hang* him!"

"WHAT?!" I yelled. "I don't *want* to be hanged!"

"Sorry, dude," said Alexia. "It's in the

dictionary, so it must be true."

"I wonder if the past tense of 'hang' is 'hanged' or 'hung'?" said Andrea.

"Who cares!?" I yelled.

"Yeah, either way, it's gotta hurt," said Neil.

"I wonder if Mr. Klutz is going to hang you by your feet or by your neck, A.J.," said Michael.

"If you get hung by your neck, your head might fall off," said Ryan.

"Yeah, but if you get hung by your feet, all the blood rushes to your head and it explodes," said Neil the nude kid.

"It's been nice knowing you, A.J.," said Ryan.

This was turning out to be the worst day since TV Turnoff Week.

The Most Amazing Trick Ever

When we got back to class after recess, there was a long wooden box in the front of the room. It looked like the kind of box that they use to bury people in.

"Welcome, ladies and gentlemen!" Miss Kraft announced. "Are you ready to witness my most amazing trick ever?"

"Yeah!" everybody shouted.

"No," I said.

"What's the matter, A.J.?" asked Miss Kraft. "I thought you liked magic tricks."

"If Mr. Klutz catches me doing one more bad thing, he's going to hang me," I told her. "So I don't want to be involved in any more tricks."

"Don't worry about Mr. Klutz," Miss Kraft told me. "I know how to take care of him."

"So what's your most amazing trick ever, Miss Kraft?" asked Neil the nude kid.

"I'm going to saw one of you in half!" she announced.

"Cool!" we all shouted. Sawing people

in half is just about the coolest thing in the history of the world.

"Where did you get that big box?" asked Ryan.

"At a big-box store," said Miss Kraft. "Okay, which one of you wants to get sawed in half?"

"Me! Me! Me!" we all shouted.

"Not me," said Little Miss Perfect. "I don't like violence."

"What do you have against violins?" I asked her.

"Not violins, Arlo," Andrea said, rolling her eyes. "Violence!"

I knew that violins and violence were two different things. I was just yanking

Andrea's chain.

"Okay," said Miss Kraft as she opened the lid of the big box, "the student who gets to be sawed in half will be . . . ANDREA!"

"Yay!" shouted everybody except for Andrea.

"Please come up to the front of the room, Andrea, and climb into the big box."

Andrea looked really mad. She was the only one who didn't want to get sawed in half, and now she was going to be sawed in half. Ha! Nah-nah-nah boo-boo on her.

At first I thought she would refuse to do it. But Andrea always does anything a grown-up tells her to do, so she went up to the front of the room and climbed into the big box. There was a hole at one end for her head to poke through.

"Are you comfy?" Miss Kraft asked Andrea. "I want to make sure you're comfortable before I saw you in half."

"Yes," Andrea said, but she sounded like she didn't mean it. She looked like she might cry.

Miss Kraft went to the closet and took out a saw. It was *gigantic*!

"Eeeeeeeeeeek!" Andrea screamed as she looked at the saw.

"Don't worry," Miss Kraft assured Andrea. "This won't hurt a bit."

"I'm scared!" said Emily, the big crybaby.

Miss Kraft started sawing the box.

Sawdust was flying everywhere. Andrea closed her eyes. The saw dug into the box.*

"I am The Great Kraftini!" shouted Miss Kraft as she pushed and pulled the saw back and forth.

"Help!" Andrea shouted. "Stop!"

"We've got to *do* something!" Emily shouted, and then she went running out of the room.

"Whew, this is hard work!" Miss Kraft said after a few minutes of sawing. She wiped her face with a tissue. Then she wiped Andrea's face with a tissue.

"Can we stop now?" Andrea begged.

---

*You should have been there!

"Stop?" said Miss Kraft. "I'm only half-way done. You know what they say: If you start a job, you should always finish it."

Miss Kraft went back to sawing for a few minutes, and then she stopped again.

"I'm tired!" she said. "Who wants to take over?"

"Me! Me! Me!" everybody shouted.

"A.J. should take over," Neil said. "He hates Andrea more than anybody."

It was true. Nobody hates Andrea more than I do. Sawing her in half would be the greatest moment of my life.

But I knew what would happen. I'd start sawing Andrea in half, and then Mr. Klutz would walk in and suspend me.

Everybody started chanting. "A.J.! A.J.! A.J.!"

"Would you like to finish sawing Andrea in half, A.J.?" asked Miss Kraft.

I *really* wanted to saw Andrea in half. But at the same time, I *really* didn't want to get into trouble again. I was faced with the hardest decision of my life.

I didn't know what to say. I didn't know

what to do. I was concentrating so hard that my brain hurt.

"A.J.," said Ryan, "if you don't want to saw Andrea in half, that must mean you're in love with her."

WHAT?!

"That's right," said Michael. "A.J., you can prove once and for all that you're not secretly in love with Andrea by sawing her in half."

"Let me out of here!" Andrea shouted. "I don't want *anybody* to saw me in half!"

"Okay," I finally agreed. "I'll do it!"

"Yay!" shouted everybody except for Andrea.

I went up to the front of the class, and

Miss Kraft handed me the saw.

"Are you sure it's going to be okay?" I asked her.

"Sure I'm sure," she replied. "Go ahead. I've done this trick a million times. Nothing can go wrong."

I started sawing the box.

"Help! Help!" Andrea shouted. "Don't do it! Stop, Arlo!"

The sawdust was flying and Andrea was screaming and everybody was hooting and hollering. This was the greatest day of my life.

"*Oooooo!*" Ryan said. "A.J. is sawing Andrea in half. They must be in *love*!"

"When are you gonna get married?"

asked Michael.

If those guys weren't my best friends, I would hate them.

"Help! No! Stop!" Andrea shouted. I was almost finished sawing through the box.

And you'll never believe in a million hundred years who walked into the room at that moment.

I'm not going to tell you.

Okay, okay, I'll tell you.

But you have to read the next chapter. So nah-nah-nah boo-boo on you.

The Return of Mr. Granite

Okay, so where were we? Oh, yeah, I was sawing Andrea in half while she was screaming and begging for me to stop. That's when *guess who* walked into the room.

Mr. Klutz! And he was madder than I had ever seen him. I thought his eyes were going to pop out of his head like in the cartoons.

"A.J.!" he shouted, grabbing the saw out of my hand. "What are you doing?"

"Uh . . . nothing," I replied.

If you get caught doing something really bad and somebody asks you what you're doing, always say "Nothing"—even if you have a giant saw in your hand and you're about to saw somebody in half. That's the first rule of being a kid.

"Sawing students in half is not acceptable behavior in school!" Mr. Klutz yelled. "That's it! I warned you several times, A.J. You are suspended . . . for the rest of your life!"

"What?! I didn't do anything!" I shouted.
"Miss Kraft! Tell him this was all your
idea!"

That's when the most amazing thing in

the history of the world happened. Miss Kraft snapped her fingers.

Well, that's not the amazing part, because anybody can snap their fingers. The amazing part was that when Miss Kraft snapped her fingers, a big puff of smoke appeared where Mr. Klutz was standing. And when the smoke cleared, Mr. Klutz was gone!

Zap! Just like that. We got to see it live and in person. You should have *been* there!

"How did you do that?" we were all asking. "Where did Mr. Klutz go?"

"A magician never reveals her secrets," Miss Kraft said. "I *told* you I would take care of Mr. Klutz."

* * *

Well, that's pretty much what happened. We didn't see Mr. Klutz for the rest of the day. I don't know where he went.

When I got home, my mom had a snack waiting for me in the kitchen.*

"How was school today?" she asked. "Did anything interesting happen?"

"Nah," I told her. "School is boring."

"You say that *every* day, A.J.," my mom said. "Interesting things *must* happen at school sometimes."

"Nope."

Well, I wasn't going to tell *her* that Mr. Granite almost died, or that I tied up Miss

---

*Well, the *snack* wasn't waiting for me. My mom was.

Kraft, or that I sawed Andrea in half, or
that Mr. Klutz suspended me and disappeared in a puff of smoke.

* * *

When I got to school the next morning, Miss Kraft was gone and Mr. Granite was back in our class. He wasn't sneezing and honking and blowing his nose anymore.

"Okay everybody," he said, "turn to page twenty-three in your math books. I've been waiting all year to do this lesson, and today we're finally going to do it."

"Uh, Mr. Granite," I said, "we did page twenty-three yesterday."

"Nice try, A.J.," said Mr. Granite. "I know you're just trying to get out of doing math, like always."

"No, he's telling the truth for once in his life, Mr. Granite," said Andrea. "We already did page twenty-three."

"Yeah," everybody said.

"Is that so?" said Mr. Granite. "Well, if you kids think you're so smart, what's eleven times eleven?"

"A hundred and twenty-one!" we all shouted.

"WHAT?!" said Mr. Granite. "How did you know that?"

"Mr. Bongo taught us," said Ryan. "He's a sock puppet."

That's when Mr. Granite did the weirdest thing in the history of the world. He went over to the window, opened it, and jumped out!

Maybe Mr. Granite will come back to class someday. Maybe we'll find out where Mr. Klutz went. Maybe people will stop blowing their noses into garbage cans. Maybe we'll get to bungee jump in the all-purpose room. Maybe Miss Kraft will stop running into doors, juggling brains, and pulling handkerchiefs out of her nose. Maybe Mr.

Bongo will become a real teacher. Maybe I'll throw my nostrils under the table. Maybe our real sub will escape from the lion's cage at the circus. Maybe we'll do another book drop. Maybe I'll get another chance to saw Andrea in half. Maybe I'll be able to talk my parents into letting me go to clown college.

But it won't be easy!